you'll fall in love with Nixie!

 Bumblebees' Bottoms!
Nixie's always getting in trouble!

A completely new kind of
fairy in fairyland.

 Rainbow Fairies meets
Horrid Henry!

Full of magical mishaps
and ingenious inventions!

A wonderfully funny story,
packed with gorgeous illustrations.

We love Nixie!

'It was fun and I would like to read more of these books.'
Rita

'a very good book . . . it is extremely funny.'
Nicole

'It's very good so I think it should go in shops.'
Keeva

'I love the story because it is full of surprises.'
Lauren

Getting to know Nixie!

FAVOURITE PLACE
Her workshop where she keeps all of her tools and does most of her of mending and making.

FAVOURITE FOOD
Lemon frosted fairy cakes, no wait, chocolate ones . . . no, toffee and banana . . . no, vanilla with a cherry on top . . .

FAVOURITE ANIMAL
Spiders—because they let her swing in their webs.

BEST FRIEND
Fizz the Wish Fairy because he always looks on the bright side.

FAVOURITE FAIRY GAME
Bursting conker cases with her magic wand so the conkers bump onto the ground.

For Annie Beth,
the original Bad, Bad Fairy,
with all my love

OXFORD
UNIVERSITY PRESS

Great Clarendon Street, Oxford OX2 6DP

Oxford University Press is a department of the University of Oxford.
It furthers the University's objective of excellence in research, scholarship,
and education by publishing worldwide. Oxford is a registered trade mark of
Oxford University Press in the UK and in certain other countries

British Library Cataloguing in Publication Data

Data available

ISBN: 978-0-19-274258-2

1 3 5 7 9 10 8 6 4 2

Printed and bound by CPI Group (UK) Ltd, Croydon, CR0 4YY

Paper used in the production of this book is a natural,
recyclable product made from wood grown in sustainable forests.
The manufacturing process conforms to the environmental
regulations of the country of origin.

THE BAD, BAD FAIRY

CAS LESTER

ILLUSTRATED BY ALI PYE

OXFORD
UNIVERSITY PRESS

Contents

Chapter 1

A BRILLIANTLY HAIRY—SCARY RIDE

★ ★ ★

ZAP! WHOOSH! A fizz of bright red fairy dust shot out of a magic wand, splattered onto a petal, and snapped it off the flower. PING!

'Gotcha!' cried Nixie the Bad, Bad Fairy gleefully.

She'd been tugging at the petal for ages.

Her face was almost as red as her dress (and even grubbier), but the petal just wouldn't break off. So she'd given up and

used magic. This was a bit risky, because Nixie's tatty black wand with its wonky red star was as naughty as she was, and it didn't always do what she wanted.

Like the time she'd tried to make a rainbow above the Enchanted Palace on the Fairy Queen's birthday. Instead of a shimmering rainbow streaming out of her wand, a bolt of lightning had shot out, hit a tower, and cracked it in half. Queen Celestine had been

very kind and understanding. The Fairy Godmother, on the other hand, had been furious.

Of course, Nixie wasn't supposed to waste magic blasting at petals. But then she wasn't supposed to be playing either. She was *supposed* to be helping with preparations for the Blossom Ball that night—like everyone else.

It wasn't that she wasn't looking forward

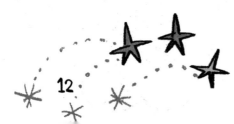

to the Blossom Ball. She was. And particularly to the party food, the magic wand games, and the prizes. *Especially the prizes*.

But it was *hours* before the Ball and it was such a perfect day for petal gliding—warm and blustery—that it seemed silly to waste it working. So she'd grabbed a coil of cobweb thread and a couple of blades of grass, and had darted up into the clear blue summer sky.

At the top of the Old Crab Apple Tree, in the middle of the Bewitched Forest, she'd found an enormous clump of blossom with petals almost as big as she was. And, because it was so high, she knew she'd be able to catch the wind and get a brilliantly hairy-scary ride.

Flying to the top of the very tall tree had been impossible and she'd almost been blown away at least twice. So she'd half flown and half scrambled through the leaves. This had been just as difficult, because there was a wild dog rose, with deadly sharp thorns, growing around the branches of the Old Crab Apple Tree. She'd torn her black tights (again) while clambering up. She was lucky it hadn't been one of her wings!

But did she care? Nope! Not now she'd got her prize. Quickly she rigged up a harness out of a sturdy piece of grass, tied it to the petal with cobweb thread, and clambered

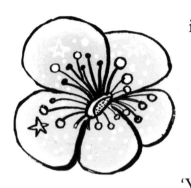

in. Immediately, a fierce gust of wind snatched at her petal glider and hurled her up into the air.

'Yahoooo!' she yelled. The blue sky spun crazily above her, and all of Fairyland whizzed round below.

'YAHOOOOOOO!'

Nobody heard her, of course. The wind whipped her tiny voice away as she spun higher and higher.

Peering down, the top of the Old Crab Apple Tree looked like

16

a huge dollop of white candyfloss, dotted with pink roses. And far below that Nixie could see the little Fairy Path zigzagging its way towards the Fairy Glade.

'Whee-heee! This is **BRILLIANT!** She clung onto the harness, kicking her legs wildly with glee.

But then the wind dropped . . .

and so did the petal . . .

and so did Nixie.

Chapter 2

A SOFT THUMP AND A PIERCING SCREAM

★ ★ ★

'Help!' she screamed. 'HELP!!!' As she plummeted down through the branches, she didn't dare open her wings in case she ripped them on a rose thorn. Slither . . . scrape . . . bump . . . bounce . . . 'Ouch! OWWWW!' She held her breath and waited for the painful CRASH! when she hit the ground. If only there was something soft she could aim for! She looked around desperately and suddenly spotted the perfect landing place.

There wasn't a **CRASH!**
There was a soft **THUMP** . . .
and a piercing **SCREAM.**

Luckily for her, she'd landed right on target.

She'd landed on Adorabella, the Goody-goody Fairy.

Adorabella had been sweeping up petals from the Fairy Path. The Fairy Queen was coming to the Blossom Ball tonight. She would drive along the Fairy Path in her royal coach, so the Fairy Godmother wanted it to be tidy.

I can't wait to tell the Fairy Godmother how good I've been, Adorabella had been thinking. *I bet she gives me a treat!*

Clearing the Fairy Path could have been a dirty job, but Adorabella had been careful not to get

21

any muck on her yellow frilly fairy dress or her sparkly satin shoes.

But now here she was, squashed and crumpled in a muddy puddle with Nixie sitting on top of her. She shoved her off angrily.

'Oops!' cried Nixie, trying to brush the mud off Adorabella's dress. But her grubby hands only made things worse, and she smeared brown streaks all down the front.

'Get off!' cried Adorabella. Her dainty yellow wings fluttered angrily and her pretty little fairy face scowled. 'You did that on purpose!' she shrieked.

'No, I didn't!' Nixie replied, trying not to laugh.

'You jumped on me!'

'I fell! Honest!'

'Well you should look where you're going.'

'I'm really, really sorry,' said Nixie, her green eyes twinkling naughtily.

'Huh!' Adorabella pouted and folded her arms. 'I bet you're not sorry at all.'

'Actually, you're right. I'm not,' said Nixie, glaring back, her little black wings buzzing crossly.

It was true. Partly because Adorabella was always getting her into trouble with the Fairy Godmother . . . and partly because Adorabella wore a yukky-yellow silly-frilly fairy dress . . . but mostly because Adorabella's yukky-yellow silly-frilly fairy dress had been absolutely the safest landing place for a fairy accidentally falling from a great height. It was just common sense—but Adorabella wouldn't understand about things like *that*.

'Look what you've done to

me,' wailed Adorabella. She really was filthy. She suddenly noticed her beautiful glittery wand had flown out of her hand and landed in the dirt.

Adorabella gasped. 'You'd better not have broken my wand,' she cried crossly.

A fairy can't do magic without a wand. They can't make rainbows, burst conkers open, or paint frost on the windows. They can't float in giant bubbles, play at who can make a feather fly the furthest, or put extra fizz in the pink lemonade . . . or do anything magical at all!

'Pick up my wand,' ordered Adorabella, stamping her foot, her angry little face going pink.

'Can't make me!' snapped Nixie, sticking out her tongue and making a rude noise.

'Right. I'm telling the Fairy Godmother.' Adorabella snatched up her dirty wand and flew off angrily.

Bumblebees' bottoms! Now I'm in trouble, thought Nixie.

Chapter 3

BiG FAT HAIRY-FAIRY FIBBER!

★ ★ ★

Tabitha Quicksilver, the Fairy Godmother, was in the kitchen of her little pumpkin house talking to the chocolate company on her Blueberry phone. Buzby, her little honeybee assistant, was busily answering BeeMails.

'No, I ordered the *party size* chocolate

fountain machine, not the *small* one . . . Yes,
it does matter! The Fairy Queen is coming
so everything must be perfect . . . Well,

obviously I can sort it out with magic, but I shouldn't have to. Goodbye!' She turned to Buzby. 'Honestly! I haven't got time for this!'

Buzby tut-tutted and waggled his antennae.

Ping-ping, ping-ping!

The timer on the cooker bleeped urgently. The Fairy Godmother rushed across to take several large trays of fairy cakes out of the oven. She set them to cool on the worktop.

Buzby smartly deleted bake fairy cakes from the blossom ball list on his LilyPad tablet. Then he read out the tasks still left to do.

'Ice fairy cakes.

Put up big party tent.

Clear petals from Fairy Path.

Make decorations.

String fairy lights on the Old

Crab Apple Tree—'

But he was rudely interrupted. The door burst open and Adorabella fluttered in, with Nixie stomping after her.

Tabitha Quicksilver nearly fell off her high-heeled shoes at the filthy state of the Goody-goody Fairy.

'Whatever happened?' she exclaimed.

Adorabella shot Nixie a dirty look. 'I was sweeping petals from the Fairy Path, *without even being asked*, when she deliberately jumped on me.'

'I didn't!'

'Yes, you did! You big fat hairy-fairy fibber!'

'Enough!' Tabitha Quicksilver rapped her

wand on the table. It was so full of magic
that a sprinkle of fairy dust escaped and iced
the cakes with a whirl of lemon frosting.
Buzby promptly deleted **Ice fairy cakes**
off the list.

'Why are you always so naughty, Nixie?'
sighed the Fairy Godmother.

'Why do you *always* think it's my fault?'

'Because it always is! Look what happened
at the Blossom Ball last year! You turned
the royal coach into a giant bubble and it
blew away—with the Fairy Queen inside!'

'That was an accident!'

This time Nixie was actually telling the
truth. She hadn't meant to turn the royal
coach into a bubble at all. She'd wanted to

make a massive bubble with the chocolate
from the chocolate fountain machine, but
the star on her wonky wand had wobbled,
and she'd missed her target and hit the
royal coach instead.

'*And* she turned *you* into a huge cupcake
with pink icing and a cherry on top,' added
Adorabella.

Nixie grinned mischievously. That hadn't
been an accident at all! Tabitha Quicksilver
shuddered at the memory.

'Nixie, say sorry to Adorabella.'

'I already did,' Nixie retorted, her wings
fizzing furiously.

'Then you won't mind saying it again,
will you?'

Nixie folded her arms and scowled, her green eyes glittering darkly.

'And it did really, really hurt!' Adorabella whined, her bottom lip trembling. Nixie rolled her eyes.

The Fairy Godmother sighed impatiently, briskly went to her magic potion cupboard, and quickly ran her eye over the coloured glass bottles:

Everyday Enchantment Potion

Very Berry Bewitching Brew

Rose Hip and Crab Apple
Entrancing Tonic

—until she got to the one she wanted:

Midnight Moonbeam
Make it Better Mixture
(strawberry flavour)

Hurriedly she gave Adorabella a spoonful.
'There. All better. Oh, it's the last drop in
the bottle!' she cried. 'Another thing to do!
But not today!' She put the empty bottle
back in the cupboard. 'Now both of you go
and clear the Fairy Path.'

'That's not fairy fair!' whined
Adorabella.

'It's as fair as a fairy godmother can make
it,' snapped Tabitha Quicksilver.

'But I don't want Nixie helping me,' moaned Adorabella.

'Good!' snorted Nixie.

'**Fairies! How is this helping?**' cried Tabitha Quicksilver. 'Run along, both of you!'

Chapter 4

PETAL TORNADO!

★ ★ ★

TING! A shower of pretty pink fairy dust fluttered out of Adorabella's wand and sprinkled onto a petal lying on the ground. It obediently flew up and put itself on top of a pile of petals at the side of the Fairy Path. It was already quite a big heap.

Strictly speaking, fairies aren't supposed to waste magic on doing chores, but using a wand is a lot easier than using a broom—

and much more fun!

TING! Another petal joined the pile.

Nixie watched her.

'You're supposed to be helping,' said Adorabella.

'It's going to take *for ever* doing them one at a time,' said Nixie scornfully. 'Move over.' She nudged Adorabella out of the way, aimed her tatty black wand, steadied the wonky star, and gave it a flick.

ZAP! VROOM! A stream of bright red sparks roared out! There was a loud **WHOOSH!** and the whole pile of petals whirled up into a mini tornado.

'Nooooo!' cried Adorabella, running over and trying to stop it. But she was

simply swept up too! She screamed and fluttered her little wings desperately, trying to escape the swirling petals. **'Put me down!'** she shrieked.

Nixie stuffed her wand in her left boot. Her bright green eyes glinted gleefully and

she did a double backflip.

Finally the tornado died down and dumped Adorabella in the same muddy puddle she'd landed in before. **SPLASH!** Nixie hooted with laughter.

Adorabella clenched her little fairy fists in fury. The whirlwind had scattered petals everywhere and now the path was even worse than when she'd started.

'Go away,' growled Adorabella. 'You are *not* helping me any more.'

'Fine!' giggled Nixie, darting off in a flash of black and red. She'd go and help the Fairy Godmother instead. You never know, she might even get a lemon frosted fairy cake.

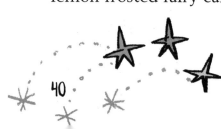

Tabitha Quicksilver was bottling pink lemonade and wild strawberry squash. They were running out of space in the kitchen, what with the chocolate fountain machine and all the trays of lemon frosted fairy cakes, so Buzby was lining the bottles up on the floor, counting them as he did so, and making a note on his LilyPad.

He jumped when the door crashed open and Nixie stomped into the kitchen.

'Adorabella won't let me help her. So I've come to help

you,' she announced, eyeing the fairy cakes.

'I'd rather you didn't,' said the Fairy Godmother, looking flustered as she gathered up a stack of bottles just as her Blueberry phone rang. Buzby picked it up.

'Thank you for calling Fairy Godmother tlc. How may I help you?' he said efficiently. 'Hold on, I'll ask.' He turned to the Fairy Godmother. 'The Meadow Fairies want to know where to put the big party tent.'

'Tell them I'm on my way!' cried Tabitha Quicksilver and she dashed out, with Buzby flitting along

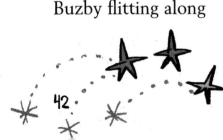

behind her. As she hurried away, she called to Nixie, **'Sit still and don't touch anything!'**

Sitting still and not touching anything were two of the things Nixie was very bad at.

Chapter 5

MIDNIGHT MOONBEAM MAKE IT BETTER MIXTURE

Nixie sat on a kitchen chair, swinging her legs in their black holey tights, bored stiff. She desperately wanted a lemon frosted fairy cake, but that would be stealing. And she knew that Buzby would have counted them. She put her chin in her hands and thought hard. What could

she do to earn one?

She suddenly remembered the empty bottle of **Midnight Moonbeam Make it Better Mixture** and a brilliant idea pinged into her head. *I'll make some more mixture! That's got to be worth a lemon frosted fairy cake. Or maybe even two.*

She opened the magic potion cupboard and looked at the bottles admiringly. They were all different shapes, with fancy silver stoppers and pretty labels. Inside the bottles the potions were all the colours of the rainbow and they glowed softly with magic.

She took the empty bottle and the recipe book, **Fifteen-minute Magic Potions,**

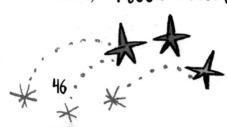

from the shelf and put them on the table. Then she helped herself to a mixing bowl and some of the Fairy Godmother's magic ingredients.

She mixed a cupful of this and a spoonful of that, then a smidge of something and a huge dollop of something else. Soon a lovely purple potion swirled in the bottom of the bowl as she stirred.

Finally she only needed to add a pinch of fairy dust to turn the mixture into a potent magical potion. Her little black wings buzzed with concentration as she gingerly picked up the pot.

She honestly meant to add just a teeny-tiny twist . . . but somehow the lid slipped

off, and before you could say **wonky wands** the whole jarful of powerful magical powder poured in!

FIZZZZZ! SPLUTTER-SPLUTTER! WHOOSH! WHIZZ!

It was like a massive box of fireworks all going off at once! Purple stars burst across the kitchen, closely followed by clusters of fizzing yellow sparks. Hundreds of tiny blue stars leapt out of the bowl and jumped around the floor like angry firecrackers.

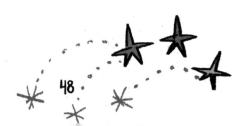

CRACKLE-CRACKLE! SNAP-A-CRACK-SNAP!

And then—

SHOOOOOOSH!

A large red star rocketed up to the ceiling and exploded—

KA-BOOM!

Silver sparkles cascaded down and instantly enchanted everything they touched! Nixie dived under the table.

Peering out cautiously, she watched in horror as the lemon frosted fairy cakes sprouted wings and flew crazily round the kitchen. The pink lemonade and wild strawberry squash bottles grew legs and chased each other all over the place. The chocolate fountain machine got the hiccups and hiccupped dollops of melted chocolate, splattering the worktop, the wall, and the floor.

'Bumblebees' bottoms!' cried Nixie. But she didn't panic. She never panicked. She often caused quite a lot of magical mayhem but she always

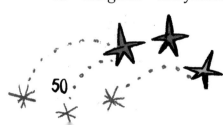

remained calm. Sometimes it wasn't even her fault—it was her wonky wand misbehaving. But Nixie knew that finding a practical way to sort things out was always safer than relying on magic!

Ducking the flying fairy cakes and dodging the sprinting bottles, Nixie grabbed the hiccupping chocolate fountain machine and plonked it in the sink.

Then she spied the empty cooling racks—they would make a perfect cage! Taking a roll of cobweb thread from the kitchen drawer,

she tied the racks together in a long line, then herded the bottles into a corner with a broom and trapped them behind the cooling racks.

Now for the flying lemon frosted fairy cakes. Grabbing a long-handled sieve,

Nixie caught them in mid-air and shoved them under the tablecloth. But soon they were fluttering up again, lifting the tablecloth with them! So she quickly darted round to each corner of the cloth and tied it firmly to the table leg underneath.

Then she grabbed her trusty spanner from her right boot, took off the back of the chocolate fountain machine, and poured all the melted chocolate into

a bowl. The machine still hiccupped, but nothing came out.

Finally she 'tidied up' as much of the splattered chocolate as she could. By eating it!

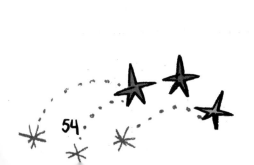

Chapter 6

NiXiE IN BiG TROUBLE

★ ★ ★

Back at the Fairy Path, Adorabella was *still* clearing up after the petal tornado. Hot, bothered, and very cross, she needed a rest. As she sat, leaning back against the soft plump stalk of a spotty toadstool, her hand touched something lying in the grass. It was a fairy wand! It was black and bent, with a wonky red

star. She snatched it up eagerly.

Aha! she thought. *If Nixie hasn't got her wand then she can't do any horrible tricks on me. Like when she turned me into a beetle . . . or when she made it snow in my*

bed . . . or when she turned my little wooden house into a gingerbread house and it went all soggy in the rain.

So she decided to hide it. *And, even better,* she thought with a smirk, *if the Fairy Godmother finds out she's lost it, she'll be in such big trouble!* She stuffed Nixie's wand down the front of her yellow frilly fairy dress. The star was a bit scratchy, but it would be worth putting up with that to see Nixie getting into a whole heap of bother.

I can't wait for the Fairy Godmother to find out that Nixie's lost her wand! she thought.

No, she really couldn't wait. So she fluttered up and zipped off to tell her.

Nixie was darting around the Fairy Godmother's kitchen, chasing the last couple of flying fairy cakes with the long-handled sieve when the Fairy Godmother and Buzby came back.

'Whatever has happened here?' cried Tabitha Quicksilver, ducking swiftly as a lemon frosted fairy cake sailed passed her and splattered onto Buzby.

'I was only trying to help,' mumbled Nixie with a face full of chocolate.

'How is this helping?' cried the Fairy Godmother. 'Stand back!' she ordered.

TINKLE-TING! A silvery stream of fairy dust showered gently from her wand and drifted across the kitchen. Everything instantly went back to where she'd left it. The cobweb thread unwound itself from the cooling racks which then flew back to the worktop where they'd come from. The bottles formed an orderly line by the cupboard again. The tablecloth untied itself from the table legs and fluttered up off the lemon frosted fairy cakes. Then the cakes skipped obediently onto the cooling racks. And all the ingredients for the **Midnight Moonbeam Make it Better Mixture** tidied themselves away in a flash of purple smoke.

'Whatever am I going to do with you, Nixie?' sighed the Fairy Godmother.

'Well, you could give me a lemon frosted fairy cake and some pink lemonade, if you like!' replied Nixie cheekily.

The Fairy Godmother reminded herself that Fairy Godmothers mustn't lose their tempers. She was slowly counting to ten in her head when the door flew open and Adorabella fluttered in breathlessly.

'Oh!' she cried, seeing Nixie. 'I didn't know you were here.'

'Well, I am, and *I'm* helping the Fairy Godmother, so there,' smirked Nixie.

Adorabella smiled sweetly at her and then pointed suddenly to Nixie's left boot and

cried, 'Nixie! Where is your wand?'

Nixie reached down to her boot for her wand—and gasped! It was gone! There was nothing in her big red boots except her little fairy feet and her trusty spanner.

Bumblebees' bottoms! Now I'm in big trouble, she thought.

Chapter 7

Missing Wand

★ ★ ★

'**O**h, for goodness' sake, Nixie!' cried Tabitha Quicksilver. 'However did you lose your wand?'

Nixie shrugged, but her little black wings drooped. Buzby buzzed in alarm.

'Have you used it today?' asked the Fairy Godmother. 'Think!'

The last time she'd used it she'd sent Adorabella whizzing up in a tornado of

whirling petals. She couldn't tell the Fairy Godmother that.

'Er . . . nope.'

'Yes, you have!' cried Adorabella, angrily flashing her yellow wings.

'Haven't!'

'Have.'

'Haven't.'

'Liar.'

'Prove it!' scowled Nixie, with her hands on her hips.

'Fairies! Please!' snapped Tabitha Quicksilver so sharply that Buzby's antennae waggled in surprise.

The Fairy Godmother closed her eyes and took a couple of deep calming breaths.

'Nixie, you must go and look for it.'

Nixie zipped off anxiously.

'She's so naughty, isn't she?' gloated Adorabella, smiling innocently.

Nixie flew back to the Fairy Path and began her search. 'Where is it?' she muttered. 'Stupid thing!'

Maybe it was under one of the petals the tornado had strewn all over the path again! Furiously she flung each and every one aside. But it wasn't there.

'Bumblebees' bottoms!' she groaned.

Just then Fizz the Wish Fairy and Fidget the Butterfly Fairy flew overhead. They'd been busily collecting petals to make garlands for the Blossom Ball and now

Fidget was struggling with her arms full of brightly coloured petals. They were heaped up all higgledy-piggledy and she kept dropping them.

'Fidget, you're hopeless!' laughed Fizz. He had stacked his petals neatly in a pile and even managed to hold them in one hand and catch the ones Fidget kept losing with his other hand.

Nixie saw her friends and called out to them. Fidget gave her a little wave and promptly dropped another petal, which Fizz caught deftly and added to his pile.

'Nixie, come and help me!' cried Fidget.

'Can't,' called Nixie. 'I've lost my wand. You haven't seen it, have you?'

They hadn't, but they darted down to help her hunt for it.

They looked between pebbles and behind toadstools and all around the Old Crab Apple Tree. Then they searched under feathers and leaves and even underneath a sleepy beetle who was lazing in the sun. But there was no sign of Nixie's wand.

'What am I going to do?' she cried anxiously.

'Don't worry,' said Fidget.

'It'll turn up,' said Fizz, giving her a cheery grin. The Wish Fairy always looked on the bright side.

'But what if it doesn't?' said Nixie worriedly.

Fidget and Fizz looked at each other in dismay. No one had ever lost a wand before!

Fairies use their wands every single day. There's always something magical that needs doing. Only this morning Fizz had mended a dragonfly's broken wing and Fidget had helped a frog get rid of the hiccups. Whatever would a fairy do without a wand?

Nixie didn't dare think what the Fairy Godmother would say. Nixie had done some very bad things . . . especially to Adorabella (who absolutely and definitely deserved them), but this was probably the worst thing she'd *ever* done.

She sighed and flew anxiously back to the Fairy Godmother's house.

In Tabitha Quicksilver's kitchen Nixie found Adorabella munching a particularly yummy scrummy-looking lemon frosted fairy cake. Nixie watched her, her wings fizzing with jealousy.

'Well, if you can't find your wand we shall have to summon the other fairies. *Someone* must have seen it,' said the Fairy Godmother. 'I *so* haven't got time for this,' she sighed under her breath. 'We simply

must find it in time for the Blossom Ball.'

Buzby selected the Fairy Call Chime app on the Blueberry phone and the tinkling summons rang out over Fairyland calling all the little fairies together.

Chapter 8

DiSASTER!

★ ★ ★

The fairies always met in the Fairy Circle. It was a ring of pretty mushrooms in a patch of emerald green grass. In the middle was a large purple and white spotty toadstool. This was Tabitha Quicksilver's special seat, and no one got to sit on it unless they'd been incredibly good, or *very bad*.

Nixie the Bad, Bad Fairy got to sit on

it quite often. She was sitting on it now, with her knee poking through a hole in her tights.

Fizz and Fidget arrived first, and then soon afterwards came Briar the Flower Fairy with Willow the Tree Fairy and Twist the Cobweb Fairy. Then the Woodland and Meadow Fairies fluttered down in a swirl of green and brown. Then the pale blue and white Winter Fairies and the rest of the fairies followed like a host of butterflies. The Tooth Fairy was last and was still in her PJs, yawning sleepily. Well, she *had* been working all night.

With a rustle of wings, all the fairies settled on the mushrooms.

74

Nixie was seething. *I'm not sitting here all day!* she thought crossly. *Not on the big toadstool in front of everyone, like an idiot!* Her friends tried to cheer her up. Fidget waved and Fizz pulled a funny face.

Then Tabitha Quicksilver spoke: 'Listen carefully. This is very important.' She paused, sighed, and then continued, 'Has anyone seen Nixie's wand?'

There was a worried buzz of wings, but everyone shook their heads.

'She's lost it!' announced Adorabella, with a smug grin.

'You big fat hairy-fairy telltale!' cried Nixie.

'I'm only trying to help.'

'Yes, of course you are, dear,' said Tabitha Quicksilver soothingly.

'No, she's not. She's just gloating because I'm in trouble!' snorted Nixie.

'Oh, really, Nixie! It's not Adorabella's fault. And why today of all days did you choose to lose your wand? You know how important it is for everything to be perfect for the Fairy Queen.' She checked her watch. 'And look at the time! She'll be on her way soon.'

'Shall I phone the Fairy Queen and delay her?' asked Buzby.

'Goodness, no!' cried Tabitha Quicksilver.

'But won't she be cross if Nixie doesn't have her wand?' asked Fidget.

'Maybe she won't notice,' said Fizz brightly.

'Of course she'll notice! How will Nixie join in the Magic Wand Welcoming Walkway or the party games without a wand?' said Tabitha Quicksilver in despair.

Nixie's little black wings drooped. The games were the best thing about the Blossom Ball, *and the prizes*, of course.

'Well, what if Nixie

79

doesn't go to the Ball *at all?*' said Adorabella sweetly.

Nixie scowled and the circle of fairies buzzed their wings angrily.

'How can Adorabella be so mean?' whispered Fizz.

'I think the Fairy Queen would notice even more if Nixie wasn't there at all!' snapped the Fairy Godmother.

Nixie was the sort of fairy people tended to notice. Rather a lot.

'This is a disaster!' cried the Fairy Godmother. 'The Fairy Queen expects every fairy to be at the Ball. How will it look if Nixie is missing?'

Adorabella was suddenly worried. She'd

only wanted to get Nixie into trouble but not the Fairy Godmother—and especially not with the Fairy Queen herself.

She thought quickly and then said, 'Wait! I *think* I might just have an idea where Nixie's wand is!' And she dashed off before anyone could ask her any awkward questions.

I knew it! She's hidden it! thought Nixie. Her green eyes glittered angrily as she sprang up to follow her, but the Fairy Godmother grabbed hold of her big red boot!

'Oh, no, you don't! You've caused enough trouble. You stay where you are.'

Fizz and Fidget looked at each other and then darted after Adorabella.

As soon as she was out of sight of the Fairy Circle, Adorabella fluttered behind a tree and anxiously wiggled Nixie's wand out of her dress.

High above her in the treetops, hidden in the blossoms, Fizz and Fidget were watching.

Chapter 9

SiLLY-FRiLLY CANDYFLOSS FAIRY DRESS!

Adorabella flew straight back to the Fairy Circle, holding up Nixie's wand for everyone to see. 'Found it!'

'Oh, thank goodness!' cried Tabitha Quicksilver. 'Where was it?'

Adorabella panicked! What could she say? She could hardly tell the truth.

But before she could say anything at all, Fizz and Fidget darted down and announced loudly, 'It was down her dress! She had it all along!'

Nixie charged at Adorabella, snatched back her wand, and then ... **WHOOSH!** Red fairy dust streaked out and Adorabella's yucky-yellow silly-frilly fairy dress turned into . . . a huge dollop of sticky yellow candyfloss! All the fairies burst out laughing.

'**HELP!** It's all prickly and itchy,' screamed Adorabella, tugging at the

candyfloss. But bits just tore off in her hand.
You could even see her frilly fairy knickers!

'Let me help,' said Nixie, grabbing a large
handful of the candyfloss dress. But that just

ripped off too! 'Oops!' she cried, looking at the chunk of sticky yellow candyfloss in her hand. It seemed a shame to waste it so she took a bite.

'Hey, it's lemon!' she mumbled, with her mouth full, and offered it to Adorabella. 'Want some?'

'No, I don't!' screeched Adorabella furiously.

'I was only trying to help!' cried Nixie, with a naughty gleam in her green eyes.

Half a dozen bumblebees buzzed over and hummed hungrily around Adorabella. They could smell the sweet sugary candyfloss. Adorabella flapped her arms frantically at them and screamed.

'Help! Get off! HELP!'

86

'Calm down!' cried Tabitha Quicksilver. 'They're not going to hurt you! Stand still and I'll magic your dress back to normal.' She raised her wand, but Adorabella suddenly took off and darted round the Fairy Circle like a demented wasp, with the bumblebees chasing her! The Fairy Godmother rushed after her.

'If you just stop, Adorabella, then I can help you. **Stop!**' she panted.

Nixie grinned wickedly and licked sticky candyfloss from her fingers. The fairies in the circle were almost crying with laughter, and Twist the Cobweb Fairy actually fell off her mushroom.

Eventually, **TING!**—with a stream

87

of silvery fairy dust, Tabitha Quicksilver managed to turn the candyfloss back into a dress, and both she and Adorabella fluttered back to the ground.

'I shall deal with you later, Adorabella,' she said sternly. Then she glanced at the time, squeaked in horror, and clapped her hands. 'Quickly, Fairies! We must get on!'

It was chaos in the Fairy Glade. Fallen petals still littered the Fairy Path and the big party tent hadn't even been put up. The fairy lights and petal garlands were

plonked in a muddled heap with the tables, and there were piles of plates, cups, and glasses everywhere. The sun was starting to set and it was beginning to get dark. How would they ever be ready in time?

But Fairy Godmothers are brilliant at dealing with calamity and catastrophe— magic or otherwise. Briskly Tabitha Quicksilver called out orders, starting with Nixie.

'Clear the petals from the path. Quickly.'

'But Adorabella was supposed to . . .' Nixie didn't even finish. Tabitha Quicksilver silenced her with a look before dashing off to sort out the tent.

89

Nixie's friends flew over to help, and they started picking up petals as fast as they could. They'd soon made a massive pile, but there were still loads left.

'This is hopeless,' said Nixie. Looking around, she spied a patch of blackberry bushes with their long sharp thorns . . . and had a clever idea.

Choosing a bramble with the biggest, sharpest thorns, some twigs, and some cobweb thread from Willow's rucksack, she built a spiky broom, which caught up the petals as she swept it across the ground.

'Nixie! That's awesome!' cried Fizz. Nixie grinned.

Flitting by to sort out the chocolate

fountain machine, the Fairy Godmother noticed the fairies clearing the petals with Nixie's brilliant spiky broom. 'Clever Fairies!' she called down, and then her

Blueberry phone rang.

Buzby dashed to answer it. 'It's the Fairy Queen!' he cried, waggling his antennae. 'The Royal Coach is just turning onto the Fairy Path! **She's nearly here!'**

Chapter 10
NOT FAIR!
★ ★ ★

Tabitha Quicksilver fluttered off to greet Queen Celestine, magically lighting the lanterns along the Fairy Path with her wand as she went.

Buzby buzzed off to sort out the food, Fidget and Briar quickly hung the petal garlands around the tables, while Nixie and Twist raced to string fairy lights on the Old Crab Apple Tree. Fizz dotted coloured

lanterns everywhere. Adorabella was busy bossing the Woodland and Meadow Fairies about.

The Fairy Queen's coach, pulled by four royal butterflies, rolled regally along the Fairy Path. Gold with a white canopy, it shone in the moonlight. Queen Celestine sat majestically inside with Tabitha Quicksilver fluttering anxiously along behind. Suddenly, **TING-A-TING!** A shower of silvery fairy dust flew from the Fairy Godmother's wand, sprinkling the Old Crab Apple Tree, and a mass of apple blossoms and rose petals fluttered around the royal coach like fireflies. It was enchanting!

Inside the party tent the fairies lined up to make an archway of wands for the grand entrance of the Fairy Queen. Gliding gracefully through the Magic Wand Welcoming Walkway, Queen Celestine smiled at each and every one of the fairies.

Her golden crown sparkled in the light from the coloured lanterns. Her long emerald wings shimmered with magic. The little fairies gazed at her in awe. Then, with a majestic sweep of her gold wand, the Fairy Queen declared the Blossom Ball could begin.

Nixie promptly helped herself to the lemon frosted fairy cake with the most icing and checked out the prizes. There was a huge bag of coloured sweeties for the winner of **Best Rainbow**, a heart-shaped bubble-blower for the **Biggest Bubble** winner, and the prize for **Bursting Dandelion Clocks** was a good-luck charm. But the loveliest prize of all, a musical treasure

box, was for **Best Dancer**. Nixie sighed. She'd never win *that*. It was hard to dance daintily in boots.

Everyone was lining up for the **Best Rainbow** game. Nixie grabbed her wand and pushed to the front of the queue. But the Fairy Godmother pulled her back.

'Not you, Nixie! The last time you made a rainbow you wrecked the Enchanted Palace!'

'Huh!' cried Nixie, stuffing her wand back into her boot. In the end Nixie didn't mind too much because Fidget won and shared the sweeties with her and the other fairies.

Nixie was sure she could win the **Biggest Bubble** prize. After all, last year she'd

97

made one as big as the royal coach! So she elbowed her way to the front again. But once more, the Fairy Godmother grabbed her back.

'No chance, Nixie! Not after last year when the royal coach *and* the Fairy Queen nearly blew away!'

'But how am I supposed to win a prize if I can't even join in?'

Tabitha Quicksilver silenced her with a raised eyebrow.

Nixie stomped off, snatched another lemon frosted fairy cake, and plonked herself down on a mushroom to watch. *What's the point of letting me come if I'm not even allowed to play?* she grumbled to herself.

Enviously she watched the other fairies blowing bubbles. Adorabella was taking it very seriously, but Fidget got the giggles and couldn't blow any at all. Twist's bubble was even bigger than Buzby, so she won the heart-shaped bubble-blower easily.

When it came to **Bursting Dandelion Clocks** Nixie was desperate to win, so she joined in before the Fairy Godmother could stop her. She blasted away with her wand in double quick time.

TING! WHOOMPH! TING-A-TING! WHOOMPH! WHOOMPH!

The air was thick with flying dandelion seeds.

She was easily the fastest. There was only one clock left.

But to her horror, instead of going **TING!**, her wand went **WHOOOSH!**, and instead of bursting, the last dandelion

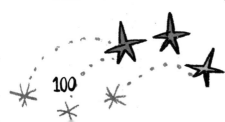

100

clock gave a little shudder and turned into

. . . a toffee apple! And everyone laughed.

'**Noooooo!**' cried Nixie. '**Stupid wand! You did that on purpose!**' And she shook it so hard that the star wobbled wildly.

Willow won the good-luck charm by just one point! 'Never mind,' he said, handing her the toffee apple. It was almost as good as winning a prize.

So Nixie took it and munched it, grinning.

So now only the dancing was left, and the musical treasure box prize. But there was

no way Nixie could win **Best Dancer**. Not with her great big boots!

Chapter 11

BEST BLOSSOM BALL ... EVER!

★ ★ ★

The music started and all the fairies sprang up and danced around daintily. Buzby joined in, doing the waggle dance. But Fizz was easily the best. He did side-slides and shuffles, backflips, and even the splits! Nixie clomped about clumsily.

'You're never going to win dancing like that!' said Adorabella, twirling past. Nixie

poked her tongue out at her. But Adorabella just pirouetted and pranced away, doing little pointy toe jumps and showing off. So Nixie kept treading on her toes, partly to annoy her but mostly because she wanted Fizz to win. Or Briar, or Fidget, or Twist— or anybody, really, just not Adorabella!

Nixie was tempted to put a spell on Adorabella's ridiculously twinkly toes— like a tripping spell or a kicking spell! That would serve her right. But she didn't dare.

She looked down at her boots. Her trusty spanner stuck out of one of them and her wand poked out of the other— giving her an idea! She could enchant her *own* boots to make them dance daintily.

I'm a genius! she thought.

SPLATTER! SPURT! Fairy dust spluttered out of her wand and onto her boots. They promptly started dancing—by themselves. All she had to do was keep up with them.

Tap tippity tap, glide, shuffle, slide . . .

Her boots were amazing! Everyone noticed, including the Fairy Queen. Round and round twirled her boots. Nixie began to think she might even win the prize.

But she should have known her wand would be up to its usual tricks. Suddenly her boots leapt up onto a chair, and then onto the table!

'Nixie, get down!' cried the Fairy Godmother. But Nixie couldn't stop!

Her boots just kept on going—squashing fairy cakes, kicking bottles, spilling drinks, and crushing table decorations. Then they danced straight up the side of the tent and up to the ceiling! Before long Nixie was upside down.

'Bumblebees' bottoms! Help!' she cried.

Everyone stopped dancing and stared up at her. The Fairy Queen was astonished.

'Nixie! Come down immediately!' ordered Tabitha Quicksilver.

But as it turned out, Nixie didn't have a choice. Her little feet slipped right out

of her great big boots and she fell! She was too busy grabbing at her wand and her trusty spanner to open her wings. She closed her eyes, held her breath, and hoped there would be something soft to land on. There was.

There was a soft **THUMP** . . . and a piercing **SCREAM.**

And for the second time that day, she landed on Adorabella!

The fairies all clustered round, trying not to laugh.

'**Oops!**' said Nixie, helping Adorabella to her feet.

But Adorabella shoved her away. 'You did that on purpose!' she screeched.

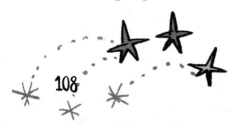

'No, I didn't!' cried Nixie, because this time it really *had* been an accident.

'You jumped on me!' shrieked Adorabella. 'I fell!'

'You're a big fat hairy-fairy fibber!' screamed Adorabella.

'And you're a big fat hairy-fairy liar!' yelled Nixie.

'Fairies, FAIRIES!' bellowed the Fairy Godmother. 'That is absolutely NOT the way to behave. Especially not in front of Her Royal Fairy Highness!'

The Fairy Queen frowned and shook her head at Adorabella and Nixie. 'I don't know which is worse,' she said, 'Nixie the Bad, Bad Fairy behaving like a Bad, Bad Fairy,

or Adorabella, the Goody-goody Fairy behaving like a Bad, Bad Fairy!' And with that she gave Fizz the musical treasure box prize for **Best Dancer**.

So Nixie the Bad, Bad Fairy didn't win any prizes at the Blossom Ball. Again. But did she care? Nope!

She'd had the **best Blossom Ball ever!**

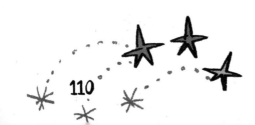

Acknowledgements

Huge thanks to:

Gaia Banks—this time for encouraging me
to pin my hopes on a fairy . . .

Annie Beth—for letting me steal so many
of her good ideas, insisting that Buzby was a boy,
and for giving me the original inspiration . . .

Kathy Webb and Liz Cross and others at OUP—
for helping me make Nixie so unique . . .

Ali Pye—for her fabulous fairy illustrations . . .

and

My boys—for being brilliant brothers to the Bad,
Bad Fairy, and starting as they meant to carry on,
with the 'No Barbie' contract.

A Little Bit About Me . . .

I used to make children's television programmes for CBBC like *Jackanory* and *The Story of Tracy Beaker*. But now I'm writing books for children instead.

This is great because it means I can spend more time with my family, and the chickens, the cats, and Bramble, my daft dog. And I get to do lots of school visits, which I love. I'm also the author of the Harvey Drew books— comedy adventures set in outer space.

I've never had a fairy costume, but I do remember being an angel in the school nativity play. I wore a long white dress and a silver tinsel halo. Unfortunately, I had a

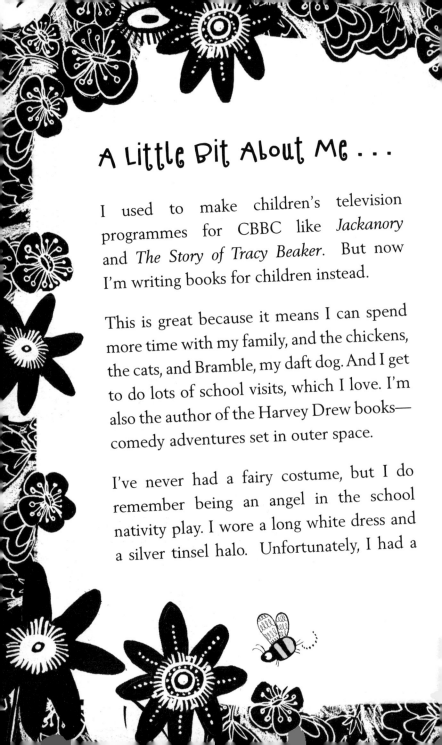

black eye, which spoiled the look a bit.
But my daughter did have a fairy costume.

It was pink and orange and she liked to wear it with wellington boots and a green plastic army hat. I thought it was a great look—and Nixie the Bad, Bad Fairy was born!

This is my favourite picture of me. It was taken by my daughter's friend when she was nine. We call it 'The Cas in the Hat'.

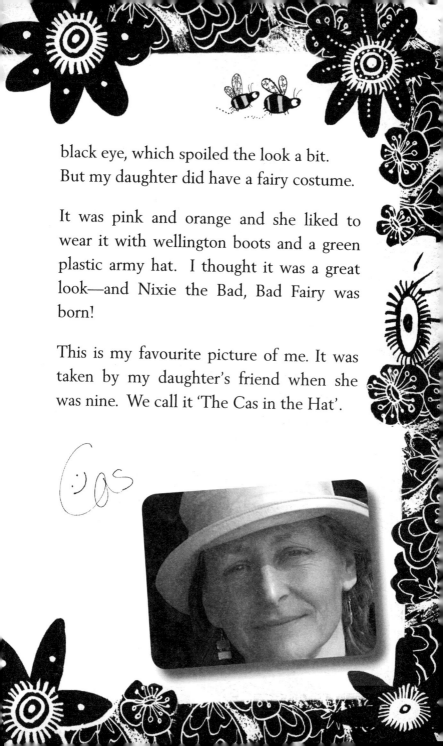

I have wanted to illustrate books for almost as long as I can remember. When I was little I spent lots of time drawing and thinking up stories. I often got told off for 'having my nose in a book' or doodling when I was supposed to be helping my family—now I have to nag my own children for exactly the same reasons!

It took me a while to achieve my ambition; I studied fashion at Central St Martins and worked as a writer before taking an MA course in illustration at Kingston University. While at Kingston, I was commissioned to illustrate *Where is Fred?* by Edward Hardy.

I have since worked for publishers including Oxford University Press, Campbell Books, Egmont, Nosy Crow, Orchard Books, HarperCollins, and Stripes. I live in Twickenham with my family and two very shy guinea pigs; I feel very lucky to do something that I love for a living.

Best wishes
Ali

YOU WILL NEED AN ASSISTANT, SO MAKE SURE THAT AN ADULT HELPS YOU.

Tabitha Quicksilver's Lemon Frosted Fairy Cakes

These delicious treats are perfect for any fairy feast.

INGREDIENTS LIST

- 125g OF CASTER SUGAR
- 250g OF BUTTER
- 2 EGGS (BEATEN)
- 150g OF SELF-RAISING FLOUR
- 1 LEMON
- 125g OF ICING SUGAR

1 Preheat your oven to 180C, gas mark 4. Then arrange 12 paper cases on a baking tray, ready for when your cake mix is made.

2 Beat the caster sugar and half the butter together until the mixture goes fluffy. Then, stir in the eggs.

3 Sift the flour into the mixture and fold in with a metal spoon. Now stir in the juice of half a lemon to give your mixture some **zing!**

4 Carefully spoon your cake mix equally into the paper cases. Now your cakes are ready to be baked!

5 The cakes will take 15 minutes to bake. When ready, they should have risen and be springy to the touch.

6 Take the cakes out of the oven and leave to cool on a wire rack. Once your cakes have completely cooled, you can add some icing. **YUM!**

7 To make the icing beat the remaining butter with the icing sugar until smooth. Then squeeze the juice from your remaining lemon half and mix with your icing.

8 Once the lemon juice is mixed in, take a spoon and spread some of the icing onto each cake.

Your cakes are finished and taste great just as they are, but if you'd like to decorate them with sprinkles or sweets do so!

Nixie's Paper Whirligig

★ ★ ★

Nixie loves things that fly, whirl, and even fall through the sky (as long as there is a soft landing). But most of all Nixie loves to make things. Use this guide to make a Nixie whirligig, and watch it spin through the air.

YOU WILL NEED:

- A SHEET OF PAPER
- SCISSORS
- A RULER
- COLOURING PENS OR PENCILS

1 On your paper, draw a rectangle, 15.5cm long and 6.5cm wide, then cut out the shape.

2 Draw out the solid and dotted lines shown in the image, then cut the solid lines that you have just drawn.

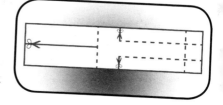

3 Draw some fairy wing shapes like the ones shown in the image and cut along the lines you've drawn, make sure you do not cut through the dotted lines on your template.

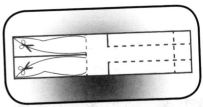

4 Fold parts A and B along the dotted lines. Folding part A towards you and part B away from you.

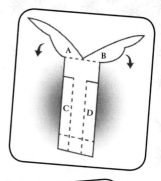

5 Now fold parts C and D.

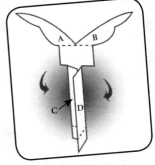

6 Fold up the bottom of your **whirly gig** as shown, and fasten with a paperclip.

7 Finish your **whirly gig** with some decoration. Try giving it some Nixie flare by drawing on some black and red stars.

Your whirligig is ready! Throw it in the air and watch it spin to the ground.

YOU WILL NEED AN ASSISTANT, SO MAKE SURE THAT AN ADULT HELPS YOU.

Fidget's Homemade Butterfly Feeder

Give some butterflies a feast with this homemade feeder.

YOU WILL NEED:

- AN EMPTY PLASTIC BOTTLE
- SCISSORS
- STRING
- 100ML WATER
- 1 TEASPOON OF SUGAR
- NAIL AND HAMMER

OPTIONAL:

- FOOD COLOURING, COLOURED PAPER, OR ACRYLIC PAINT FOR DECORATION.

1 Get started by asking your assistant to help you cut the bottom third off of your plastic bottle with scissors.

2 Then cut petal shapes into the bottom of the plastic bottle.

3 With the help of your assistant punch a hole in each side of the bottle with scissors, and thread a long piece of string through these holes, so that the string can later be tied and hung up outside.

4 The next step is tricky, ask your assistant to make a small hole in the lid of the plastic bottle, the easiest way to do this is with a hammer and nail. Then thread a piece of string through the hole in the bottle cap. Tie a knot in the string so that it won't fall through the hole. Then screw the cap back on tightly.

5 Now it's time to make some butterfly nectar. In a jug mix 1 teaspoon of sugar with 100ml of water. If you want, you can add food colouring to the nectar, the bright colour will attract more butterflies.

6 Before you add the nectar to your feeder, it's time to get creative, and make your butterfly feeder really stand out! You could try cutting flower shapes out of coloured paper and sticking them to your feeder, or painting bright patterns onto the bottle, adding a splash of colour, just like Fidget the Butterfly Fairy would.

7 Carefully pour your nectar into your feeder then hang up outside. Now your feeder is complete, ready for any hungry butterflies that pass by.

This activity works best between April and September, as butterflies hibernate in colder months.

There's plenty of mischief to be had in Nixie's next adventure. Turn the page for a taste of what's to come . . .

'SNOW!' whooped Nixie the Bad, Bad Fairy excitedly, looking through her wonky little window at the most enormous white snowflakes tumbling down outside.

She was still in bed, so she threw off her quilt and leapt up. Her little black wings buzzing eagerly against her torn and tatty red fairy dress.

'Yippee! The Winter Fairies have been!' she cried, and her green eyes glittered with glee as she flitted a double back somersault!

At this time of year the Winter Fairies magically scatter frost on the windows of the fairy houses, hang icicles in the trees, put ice on the Polished Pebble Pond, and cover everything with a thick blanket of fresh, white snow. Fairyland becomes a beautiful winter wonderland. But for Nixie, it's a wonderful winter . . . playground!

'YA-HOOOOO!!!' she yelled, 'sledging . . . skating . . . and snowball fights!'

Hurriedly clambering into her big red clompy boots, Nixie grabbed her scarf and crammed her woolly hat onto her black spiky hair.

Then she shoved her wonky black wand into her left boot, so hastily that the red star on the end wobbled about madly, and stuffed her trusty spanner into the other boot. Flinging open her shabby wooden front door, she charged outside.

'WA-HOOO!' she hooted, stamping and stomping deep footprints into the snow. Crisp and crunchy underfoot, but soft and fluffy underneath, it was perfect for snowballs. She scooped up a handful of it, squidged it together, and hurled it as far and as hard as she could.

Wheeee . . .

Love Nixie? Then we know you're going to enjoy reading about these fantastic characters too . . .